Dear Parent:

Your child's love of re

Every child learns to read in a different way and at his or her own speed. Some go back and forth between reading levels and read favorite books again and again. Others read through each level in order. You can help your young reader improve and become more confident by encouraging his or her own interests and abilities. From books your child reads with you to the first books he or she reads alone, there are I Can Read Books for every stage of reading:

SHARED READING
Basic language, word repetition, and whimsical illustrations, ideal for sharing with your emergent reader

BEGINNING READING
Short sentences, familiar words, and simple concepts for children eager to read on their own

READING WITH HELP
Engaging stories, longer sentences, and language play for developing readers

READING ALONE
Complex plots, challenging vocabulary, and high-interest topics for the independent reader

I Can Read Books have introduced children to the joy of reading since 1957. Featuring award-winning authors and illustrators and a fabulous cast of beloved characters, I Can Read Books set the standard for beginning readers.

A lifetime of discovery begins with the magical words **"I Can Read!"**

Visit www.icanread.com for information
on enriching your child's reading experience.

For Mia
—S.W.

To Nash, Peter, and Millie
—A.W.

Sketty and Meatball
Text copyright © 2024 by Sarah Weeks
Illustrations copyright © 2024 by Alex Willmore
All rights reserved. Manufactured Malaysia.
No part of this book may be used or reproduced in any manner whatsoever without written permission except in the case of brief quotations embodied in critical articles and reviews. For information address HarperCollins Children's Books, a division of HarperCollins Publishers, 195 Broadway, New York, NY 10007.

www.icanread.com

Library of Congress Control Number: 2023943940
ISBN 978-0-06-243162-2 (trade bdg.) — 978-0-06-243161-5 (pbk.)

Book design by Marisa Rother

24 25 26 27 28   COS   10 9 8 7 6 5 4 3 2 1   First Edition

Sketty and Meatball

BY Sarah Weeks   PICTURES BY Alex Willmore

HARPER
An Imprint of HarperCollinsPublishers

Sketty and Meatball
do everything together.
They play together.
They bark together.

Sketty and Meatball run and jump
and roll in the grass together.
If Sketty sniffs a flower,
Meatball sniffs a flower too.

If Meatball wags his tail,

Sketty's tail is wagging too.

When Sketty and Meatball get tired

of running and jumping

and sniffing flowers,

they curl up together

under the lemon tree

and take a nice, long nap.

"What shall we do today?"
asks Sketty.
"We can roll in the grass,"
says Meatball.

"We did that yesterday,"
says Sketty.

"We can bark at that cat,"
says Meatball.

"We did that yesterday too,"
says Sketty.
"Let's find something new to do."

"Are you thinking
what I'm thinking?"
asks Meatball.
"I hope so," says Sketty.

"Let's go to the dog show!"
say Sketty and Meatball
at the same time.

There are lots of dogs
at the dog show.
Lots and lots and LOTS of dogs.

There are short dogs with long tails.

And long dogs with short tails.

17

There are big dogs
with little spots.

And little dogs

with big spots.

There are silly dogs in long coats.

And chilly dogs in short coats.

Hairy dogs

and scary dogs

and very hairy scary dogs.

Meatball sees a tiny dog
with a big red bow on her tail.
Sketty sees a big red dog
with a tiny hat on his head.

They see lots and lots of dogs.

"Look!" says Meatball.

"That dog looks like you only smaller!"

"Look!" says Sketty.

"That dog looks like you only bigger!"

"What kind of dogs
do you like best?" asks Meatball.

"Are you thinking what I'm thinking?"
asks Sketty.

"I hope so," says Meatball.

25

"Hot dogs!" say Sketty and Meatball
at the same time.

The dog show is lots of fun.

Sketty and Meatball are tired.

"Are you thinking what I'm thinking?"
asks Sketty.

"I hope so," says Meatball.

29

"We could curl up together
under the lemon tree
and take a nice, long nap.
What do you think?" asks Sketty.
Meatball does not say anything.

Meatball was thinking

the same thing too.